Thick as Thieves

A Brief Encounters novella

By Cyan Tayse

Thick as Thieves

A Note For The Reader

This story may contain triggers.
If you or anyone you know suffers from depression, anxiety or abuse, please seek the guidance of a mental health professional.

And remember, be kind, always. You never know what troubles someone is going through behind closed doors.

Helpline 1: (09) 522 2999
Helpline 2: 0800 111 777
Website: WWW.LIFELINE.ORG.NZ/

Chapter One

Leo

"This the place?" A cigarette hangs from my lips as I stare up at the two-storey mansion across the street.

Skeet pulls out a crumpled piece of paper and squints at the ink in the darkness. "Sixty-eight Braebrook Drive." He nods, stuffing it back in his pocket. "Yup, this is the one."

With one last drag of my smoke, I walk across the road, flicking the remnants in the gutter as I pass. That familiar surge of adrenaline floods my body as I prepare to break into this shiny new home, complete with the 'latest in security' kindly supplied by my counterpart, Mario. With his lack of tatts, and his square, chiselled jaw, he's the only one of us who could pass for a good, wholesome lad. The suckers in these flash new subdivisions always fall for his charm and let him into their homes under the pretence he's making their homes safer. When really, he's making sure we have easy access to all their riches. We have an override in the system making it impossible to be detected. We're in and out before anyone notices. And we never hit the same area twice in a month. Always keep moving so we don't draw any attention.

This place is no different. Skeet hooks up the override software and within a matter of seconds, he gives a thumbs up. I wait a beat before placing my hand on the handle and pushing down. The door swings open on silent hinges. We're in.

A glance at my watch tells me we have exactly forty-three minutes until the Van der

Kley's will return from their monthly committee meeting. Plenty of time to extract what we need.

Unlike other petty thieves, we only go after the small things that won't be missed. A necklace here, a trinket there. Things that could easily be misplaced or go unnoticed for a good length of time. It may be playing it safe, but we can't risk anything linking Mario to the thefts, not when he is our way in.

The Van der Kley's are well known in the area for their love of art. They were the drive behind the new art gallery's construction, Mrs Van der Kley having her very own wing to display her works. Strolling down the hall of their home, I can see why. The walls are adorned with framed prints and canvases, and hello, what do we have here? A journal? I flick through the pages. *This could make for interesting reading.* Shoving it in my bag, I take one last look at the paintings on the wall.

They're good, but not what we're here for. No, that would be too obvious. What we want is much smaller and inconspicuous. A diamond encrusted ornament sits on a dusty shelf in her studio, tucked in behind a photo of her shaking hands with the Prime Minister. Judging by the state of the shelf, I doubt they'll notice it anytime soon, if at all.

With the ornament safely wrapped in a silk scarf and tucked into my rucksack, I quickly scan the rest of the house, searching for any other goodies we could pilfer.

The master bedroom is almost as big as my entire house. They even have a lounger in one corner. A king-size bed sits in the centre of the room, under a long, thin window. There's an en-suite to the left, and a walk-in-robe to the right. I head for the wardrobe, hoping to find some hidden jewellery.

Row upon row of shoes adorn the back wall, with either side holding a myriad of coats and jackets. Immediately to my left is a set of drawers filled with more clothes. Rummaging through, I come up empty handed. I swing the torch back to the coats. Something draws me to them, but I can't quite put my finger on it. If I've learned anything through the years though, it's to follow my gut.

I push the coats aside, running my hand down the wall behind them. All feels smooth and normal until my fingers graze across a tiny lip in the paintwork. "A secret compartment." A smile spreads across my face. "Jackpot."

Thick as Thieves

Chapter Two

Alexander

There's someone in the house. There's someone in the freakin house! The one time I don't go with them to their stupid committee meeting...

Thud.

"Shit," I hiss under my breath. "What should I do?" Peering around my room full of books, I regret not being more of a team sports kind of guy; a baseball bat would come in handy about now. Maybe I should just call the cops, let them deal with whoever is prowling around my home. Yes, that's what I'll do. I reach for my phone, only to remember I left it out in the lounge, charging. *Damn it.*

Okay, new plan. Man up and defend your territory. You're a force to be reckoned with. You're a Van der Kley for Christ's sake.

I hate that my father's voice is what jolts me into action, but it does. With shaking hands, I push the sheets back and swing my legs over the edge of my bed. I've never really been one for confrontation, but I can't just sit here and wait for them to find me. At least this way, I have the element of surprise on my side.

On silent feet, I move around the bed to find my jeans. Probably not the best idea to approach a potentially dangerous person in just my boxer briefs. Or is it? Maybe a half-dressed man is scarier than a fully clothed one. Or maybe I'm just stalling for time. I can't be sure which it is anymore.

I don't have time to make my mind up because the sound of footsteps marching down the hall stops me in my tracks. I tip-toe across the room and blindly reach out in the dark, trying to find something that will work as a weapon.

The footsteps stop right outside my door, and my heart threatens to beat itself right out of my chest. It's funny, I should be used to this by now, but I'm not. This is different. This is the unknown behind my door, not the man who haunts my dreams.

I hold my breath, hoping they'll just leave and I won't have to confront them at all.

All hope is shattered when I hear the most terrifying thing in the world. A hand grasping the handle of my door, and a voice rasping out, "There's someone in there."

Thick as Thieves

16

Chapter Three

Leo

"You sure?"

Skeet nods his head once. I hand him the few things I've gathered and motion for him to leave. Our little enterprise doesn't work without him and his software, so he needs to be well away when the cops show up. He hesitates, not willing to leave a man behind. "Go," I mouth, not budging from my spot. When he turns on his heels, I give him a ten-second head start before I wrench the door open.

"Don't come any closer!" I pause in the doorway, taking in the half-naked guy before me. *Hello, sailor.*

"I mean it! I-I've got a weapon!"

My eyes land on the 'weapon' in question, and I fold my arms across my chest with a smirk. "Is that one of those foam swords kids get at a Crusaders game? I think I'll take my chances."

He stumbles backwards, his eyes darting to his sword and back again. "Shit." He tosses it to the floor and brings his fists up. The kid's got balls, I'll give him that.

"You don't wanna do that."

He juts his chin up and narrows his eyes. "Don't I know you?"

"I doubt it."

He drops his arms. "No, I do. You're one of the mafia boys. You always sit up the back of class." *Shit.* Mario's suggestion to carry masks doesn't seem like such a dumb idea anymore. I wasn't counting on being seen at all, let alone recognised. Before, I was a threat, now, I'm just a guy he knows from school. Still, I take the bait. The longer I can stall him, the more chance Skeet has of getting away.

"Mafia boys?" I raise my brow.

"You know, petty criminals." He waves his arm around the room. "Clearly it's an accurate description seeing as you're in my home, uninvited." He folds his arms across his chest, and I don't miss the bulge of his bicep. *Dude must work out.*

I shrug. "Clearly. And you're the little brown-noser who always sits in the front."

His jaw drops, and he rolls his eyes, placing his hands on his hips. "Think what you want, but I'm not going to apologise for being studious. You can't be a doctor without getting good grades. At least *I'll* be doing something worthwhile when I leave this town. What'll you be doing? Knocking over a corner dairy for a pack of smokes? Selling drugs? Or maybe you'll be sitting in a jail cell wondering where it all went wrong." He smirks, and damn if it isn't sexy as hell. Too bad he's in need of an attitude adjustment.

"Oh, I see. You think you're better than me because you got dealt a good hand. Born into this hoity toity lifestyle, having everything handed to you on a silver platter. But you know what?" I poke a finger at his chiselled chest. "You wouldn't last two seconds in my world."

"Who says I want to?"

I nod at his stance. "You did, when you challenged me."

His throat bobs as he swallows, and his bravado diminishes somewhat. The look in his eyes is one of defeat, but he brings his fists back up all the same. "Alright. Come on then."

I shake my head. "I'm not going to fight you."

"What? Wh-why not? It's what you do, right?"

I quirk an eyebrow, the corner of my lip pulling up slightly. *This guy.* "Yeah, it's what *I* do. But it sure as shit ain't what *you* do. It wouldn't be a fair fight."

He straightens up, a look of confusion marring his face. "How do you know I haven't taken martial arts or something? I could be a black belt for all you know."

I can't help the chuckle that slips from my lips as I take a step forward. "One." I hold up a finger. "Anyone who's done martial arts knows it's about self defence and not about trying to start something." I take another step forward, holding up a second finger. "Two, anyone who's actually thrown a punch knows that that is the best way to break your damn thumb." I nod at his hand then hold my own fist in the air. "You throw a punch with it tucked inside your palm like that and you'll know about it." Reaching out, I pull his thumb from his enclosed fist and position it. "Like this."

He stares at our hands then lifts his eyes to meet mine. "I… um… thanks?"

I pat his cheek with the palm of my hand. "Anytime, doc." I let my eyes linger on his for a beat before I turn on my heels and saunter out the door.

"Wait!"

I pause, tipping my head to show I'm listening.

"Aren't you worried I'll call the cops?"

Pulling my smokes from my pocket, I take my time selecting one and lighting it before I answer. "You and I both know that's not gonna happen." I step through the door, blowing a puff of smoke in his direction before settling my gaze on his growing arousal. "You need a little help with that?"

His hands quickly fly to cover himself, and the look of terror in his eyes is priceless. *Got him.*

I take another drag of my cigarette, puffing smoke rings in the air. "Don't worry." I wink. "I won't tell if you don't."

Chapter Four

Alexander

With a deep breath, I lift my head and stride through the entrance to class. I purposely keep my eyes trained on the whiteboard at the front. The last thing I need is to see those eyes of blue staring back at me, reminding me of my little embarrassment the other night. And even though I know it would be foolish for him to tell anyone and incriminate himself, I still find myself waiting for the sneers of my classmates. I've managed to keep my attraction to men a secret, and I'd like to keep it that way. At least until I get out of this small town where everyone thinks it's their business to know your business.

It's been easy to hide it up until now. No one has grabbed my attention like Leo. Maybe it's the bad-boy vibe he has going on, or maybe it's the way he refused to fight me, knowing I'd lose. Or perhaps it's because he's everything my father would despise. Whatever it is, I can't let it distract me from my studies. My grades are my ticket out of here; not just this town, but out from under my father's watchful eye.

To everyone else, he is this upstanding citizen who runs his own business and donates his time and money to charities. But they don't see what he's like behind closed doors. The tyrant he becomes when he's had one too many drinks. Even my own mother has no idea what he's capable of.

For as long as I can remember, he's dropped snarky remarks my way, always out of Mum's earshot. He waits until she's in her studio with her music up, immersed in her art. That's when he comes to my room. At first, he'd find any excuse to yell at me and that would be the extent of it. But over the years he became angrier and more daring. He'd force me to my knees while he belittled me. Sometimes he'd backhand me, other times he'd use his fist or worse. Always to the ribs or back though, never somewhere visible.

I have no idea what I did to make him hate me so much, and I don't care. All I want is to be free of him.

Three more months. Three more months and I can get out and never look back. Only then can I be who I really am.

"Alexander?" I blink, looking up from the paper I'd been doodling on. Mr Hollings is standing beside my desk with a note in his hand. "Miss Holt would like to see you in A Block."

"Oh, okay." I take the note and stuff it in my bag with the rest of my books, glad for the excuse to leave.

When I reach A Block, Miss Holt greets me with a smile. "Alexander, it seems your reputation precedes you." I quirk my brow in question, and she continues. "I have a student who has requested you as an English tutor. His grades are fine, but he needs a little help on his essay writing." She walks around her desk, taking a seat. "I know you have a heavy workload this year, but if you're up for the challenge, it will look great on your references for college."

Anything that can give me an advantage on my college applications is a win in my book. Dropping my bag to the floor, I pull up the seat across from her desk. "Sure, Miss Holt. I would love to help."

"Excellent. I'll introduce you, and then I'll leave it to you to work out a suitable schedule." She presses a button on her desk and speaks. "Send him in please."

There's a crackle of interference and then a voice replies, "Right away, Miss Holt."

The door opens, and I turn to see who I'll be tutoring. All the air seems to vanish from the room as my eyes land on those unforgettable seas of blue, and suddenly I can't breathe, I can't move, I can't hear. All I can do is stare at the bluest eyes I've ever seen. The eyes belonging to Leo.

Thick as Thieves

Chapter Five

Leo

The look on his face when I step in the room is something between intrigue and shock. From our little altercation the other night, I'm ninety-nine percent sure he's into me. The other one percent has its doubts. For all I know, he could be an adrenaline junky, getting hard on the thrill of fighting off an intruder. We all have our quirks I guess, and apparently, mine is an overachieving rich dude. Talk about opposites attract.

"Leo, welcome." Miss Holt beckons me in further. "Come and take a seat."

I clear my throat, bobbing my head in Alexander's direction. "How's it going?" Dropping my bag by the door, I pull up the seat next to him.

"Uh…" He shifts in his seat making it easier for me to get a better look at his face. "Good, thanks."

It's funny how you can see someone every day and never really notice them. But the glimpse I got at his washboard abs the other night, combined with the way he's looking at me right now with those intense whiskey coloured eyes is enough to make me sit up and take notice. Alexander may be a goody two-shoes, but he's also a hottie.

The seconds tick by and we continue staring at each other while Miss Holt organises some forms to fill in. It's not until she perches on the front of her desk that we look away.

"Here." She hands me a piece of paper. "You need to fill this in to get the tutoring under way. Alex," she turns to him, "I have you down as having fifth period free on Wednesdays, yes?"

"Uh, uh, y-yes, Miss Holt, that's right," he stammers. It's hard to believe he's the one who'll be tutoring me when he can barely string two sentences together.

"Does that work for you, Mr Ryder?"

Flashing my teeth with a wink, I nod. "Sure thing, Miss."

She claps her hands together, steepling her fingers on her lap. "Excellent. Once we've got the paperwork filled in, you can make a start. Maybe see if you have any other corresponding free periods." Pushing off from her desk, she sashays to the door, pulling it open. "Thank you, gentlemen. If you hurry, you can make it back for the second half of class."

Alexander practically runs out the door while I follow behind, getting an unobstructed view of his ass. There is no way he has an ass like that without working out. Definitely more to this pretty-boy than meets the eye.

Chapter Six

Alexander

I should be writing a book report on *Lord of the Flies*, but I can't stop thinking about Leo. What's his game? Why would he ask me to tutor him? I can't shake the feeling he's out to expose my secret. But why?

I can't think of one reason this would benefit him, unless... Unless I stopped him getting what he needed the other night. Maybe he's out to bribe me for what he was really after. From what I can tell, nothing is missing. Mum's paintings are still along the hall, and they're worth a pretty penny. Other than company shares, the only other thing worth any money would be my mother's jewellery or my parents' Audi. The car was with them that night, and Mum hasn't mentioned any missing jewellery, which means he still needs to get what he came for.

Shit.

My throat goes dry and the collar of my shirt feels like it's tightening. I'm not cut out for this. All I want is to get out of this town unscathed, but it's seeming less and less like that's in the cards for me. With a father who hates me on one side and a thug who no doubt has plans for me on the other, I'm beginning to think I'm cursed.

When the bell rings and I walk out the door, I find Leo leaning against the lockers, waiting for me. He has that perpetual smirk on his face like he has a private joke with the universe. And even though I know he's out to get me, I can't help the jolt my heart makes at the sight of him. My eyes involuntarily flit to his hands, igniting the memory of them touching mine, and I almost groan out loud. Almost.

Hold it together, Alex.

He nods his head, kicking off from the wall to walk alongside me. I don't speak, and neither does he. We just walk in an awkward silence, our shoulders occasionally bumping against each other. My mind goes into overdrive trying to think of something intelligent to say, but I'm struck speechless by the warmth radiating off his body. This guy who wasn't even on my radar has suddenly become the only thing occupying my mind. His scent, his hands, his eyes, and that damn sexy smirk.

We pull up outside my next class and he grabs my hand, slipping a piece of paper into my grasp before turning away. His hand sweeps through his hair then up into a wave of sorts, and I swear I can hear the deep rumble of his laughter.

Tearing my eyes from his departing figure, I look down at the piece of paper in my hand, unsure whether to be elated or petrified. Only one way to find out.

Alex

Meet me at the park, 7pm

Leo

Petrified. Definitely petrified.

Chapter Seven

Leo

With an armload of groceries, I push through the front door. "Mum? I'm home." The television is on low with some kids' cartoon playing, and Zack has his eyes glued to the screen. "Hey, buddy." I run my free hand through his hair before placing the groceries on the bench. Peeling my jacket off, I hang it on the hook by the door. "Where's Mum?"

"Bedwoom," Zack says. "She sweeping."

"Yeah? You been good for her?"

He nods his head, his eyes wide. "Uh-huh. I beed vewy quiet." He brings his finger up to his lips. "Shhh."

Shit, shit, shit. Not again.

"That's good, buddy." I grab a bag of popcorn and pour some into a bowl for him. If Mum is having another one of her episodes, there's no telling when he last ate. "Here, eat up. I'll fix you some dinner shortly, okay?"

His eyes light up as he grabs the bowl from my hands, his chubby fingers plunging straight in for a handful. "Mmmm."

"I'm gonna go check on Mum, okay? You stay here and watch your programmes."

"Mmhmm."

I trudge down the hall, my feet feeling as though they have lead in them the closer I get to her room. In my haste to get to school this morning, I'd neglected checking in on her. If I'd known she was having an episode, I never would've left Zack here with her.

"Mum?" I knock gently on her door. When I get no response, I push it open, peering through the darkness. "Mum?"

The blinds are pulled closed, and the air feels hot and stuffy. Dodging the piles of discarded clothes, I make my way across her room to let some air in through the window. "That's better," I mumble half to myself. It's likely I won't get any kind of response from her, but I can't seem to help myself from trying every time. "Mum?" I perch on the edge of the bed. The duvet is scrunched in a ball in the middle of the bed, and the only signs she's even in here and still alive, are the tiniest of movements signalling her breathing. Placing my hand somewhere in the middle, I give a gentle shake. "Mum? You wanna come out and have something to eat?"

No response.

"Zack's eating some popcorn, but I bought us some mince for dinner. I'm going to make your favourite, Spaghetti Bolognese."

The pile of bedsheets lifts in an exaggerated sigh, but still she doesn't say a word.

"Have you eaten today?" I try again, giving her more of a nudge.

Nothing.

With a sigh, I stand, knowing this could go on for days. "Okay, well, I'm going to go make a start. We'd love to see you out there. Just when you're ready." I hover just a little longer, willing her to get up and say something, anything, but it doesn't happen. Pausing in the doorway, I whisper, "Zack needs you, Mum. He loves you." I sigh, raking my hand through my hair. "We both do."

Chapter Eight

Alexander

"What's the matter, Alex? Aren't you hungry?" Mum asks as I push the food around my plate.

"Not really, no." I shake my head. "Can I please be excused?" My stomach has been in knots ever since Leo handed me that note.

"Of course, sweetheart." Mum pats my hand. "I hope you're feeling okay."

"Mmm, just tired. I might go for a walk, get some fresh air." Carrying my plate to the kitchen, I spy the empty bottles of beer on the bench and hope to God Dad leaves me alone this time. I step around the table, avoiding my father's glare, focusing only on putting one foot in front of the other. A glance at the clock on the wall tells me it's 6:30pm. Half an hour.

Meet me at the park, 7pm.

Aside from giving me a beat down, or demanding I pay him out for his losses, I can't think of any other reason why he'd want to meet me in the park, after dark.

A shudder runs down my spine. Part of me is scared shitless, but there's also this small part of me, way deep down in the pit of my belly, that's also a little excited to see him again. I don't understand what's going on with me lately. How can I be so obsessed with someone who scares me?

Daddy issues. Perhaps, subconsciously, I want someone powerful like him? Ugh, just the thought makes me feel ill. He's made my life a living hell, so why would I want that in any shape or form? No, it has to be something else. I refuse to believe that my fucked-up psyche is telling me I want someone even remotely like my father.

He could save you. Yeah, that's more likely. Not that I *need* saving. I've done fine on my own so far, and I've only got another few months until I'm finished school and out of here for good. But, the idea of someone standing up to him for me? Now *that* is a turn on. Just once I'd like to see *him* cower in fear. I'd like to see someone tell him *he's* not good enough as a man, let alone a father.

But is Leo really the one to do that? He's a mafia boy. A rebel without a cause. And a rebel isn't exactly what a doctor needs by his side.

Maybe not a doctor, but a writer… I push that thought down with all the others. As much as my mother would love to see me embrace my creative side, I can't allow myself that freedom. To write the tales that weave inside my head would be too tempting, too revealing, too much of *me* on display for the world to see. I'm not ready for that. Not now, maybe not ever.

Doctor Alexander Van der Kley, however, has a safe and stable ring to it. It's fitting of the Van der Kley name, and it's what I've been conditioned to train for, whether I wanted it or not. To be honest, I don't even remember who first suggested it, me or my father. Perhaps it was said on a whim one day, and the seed was planted. I don't even care anymore. All I know is it's my ticket out of here.

Music flows through the house almost the instant I step foot in my room to grab my shoes. Judging by the look on my father's face, I've only got a few minutes to get out before he finds me. Thankfully, my trainers are right where I left them, beside the bed. I sit down, pulling them on in one fluid motion. Bending down, I tie them as fast as I can – but not fast enough, it seems. The door to my room opens and closes, and my father's shoes come into my line of sight. The stench of alcohol wafts around me, and I brace for what's about to come.

It takes everything I have not to shrink back from his intense stare. Instead, I concentrate on my laces, taking my time.

"You're hiding something." The sound of his belt being pulled from the loops on his pants rings in my ears, and my throat goes dry. He hasn't used the belt in a few months. Not since I got a B on my maths test.

Knowing there's no correct answer, I sit up, meeting his eyes. "No, Sir."

"And now you're lying. I don't tolerate liars. *Van der Kley's* do *not* lie." He doesn't raise his voice, but his tone holds malice. Over the years, he's perfected the art of intimidation. "Stand up."

I do as I'm told, even though my legs threaten to buckle beneath me. There's no point in fighting. When he gets like this, he'll find any excuse to bend me to his will.

"Turn around."

I do so, removing my shirt and bending slightly, before he has to ask. If I'm compliant, he doesn't hit as many times.

I hear the whoosh of the belt through the air almost at the same time it connects with my back. Fighting the urge to run, I suck in a breath and wait it out. One, two, three lashes before the belt loop hits the floor.

"Van der Kley's don't lie. Remember that." *If that were true, he'd be in a jail cell right now.*

I don't move while he threads his belt back through his pants. It's only when I hear the click of the door closing behind him that I dare to breath again. My back throbs in time with my heartbeat, and I stifle a sob. I refuse to let him see me cry.

My feet shuffle across the floor towards my bathroom. Every tiny movement sends a jolt through my back, but I grit my teeth and push through. It's almost 7pm, and I can't risk standing Leo up.

With the stark light of the bathroom lamp, I get a good look at the welts across my back. Red and inflamed, they criss-cross in the same lines as last time. I know because I can barely see the scars.

Pressing a cold washcloth to the bits I can reach, I hiss beneath my breath, "Shit." Putting a shirt on is not going to be fun, but I can't exactly leave the house like this. My face is covered in a fine sheen of sweat, and the welts are beginning to weep. I'm a hot mess.

I grab a light cotton, button-up shirt and ease my arms in slowly. The fabric clings to my back, and I know it's going to sting when I eventually peel it back off again, but I can't think about that now. The park is at least a five-minute walk from here, longer if you account for the shuffling, and it's now 6:57pm.

I slip out the door with my head down and hands in my pockets. If I'm going to get a beat down, I may as well get it over with.

Chapter Nine

Leo

He's late.

I kick a clump of dirt across the field, watching it land a hundred metres away.

Maybe he's not coming.

To distract myself, I slam the back of my heel into the ground until I get another clump of grassy dirt. I step back, eyeing up the mass as if it is a rugby ball and I'm about to kick it through the posts. My eyes land on the space ahead, and I calculate the angle I need to hit to get it there. A step to the left, a shuffle back. I line it up and watch it fly through the air, narrowly missing the kid walking towards me like he's shit himself. He jumps out of the way, his face contorting in pain as if it had actually made contact.

Interesting.

Folding my arms across my chest, I stand back, watching. Something's not right. I know he's scared of me, but he's never looked like *that* before. Like he's a mouse walking into a lion's den.

I walk towards him, nodding my head to the bench seat between us. Sitting on one side, my forearm braced on my knee as I pull my Marlboro's from my pocket, I keep one eye firmly on his face. He has sweat pouring off him, as if he's run a bloody marathon. With a body like his, there's no way he's that unfit.

He stops in front of me, his hands in his pockets and his eyes lowered.

I drag a cigarette out with my teeth then hold the pack out towards him. "You want one?" He shakes his head, so I push it back in my pocket and grab my lighter. "You gonna stand there all night, or you gonna sit down?"

"What do you want, Leo?" *Someone got their balls back.*

I lean back, running my arm along the back of the seat. "I just want to talk, that's all."

"That's it?"

"Yeah. Why? What'd you think was gonna happen?"

He toes the ground with a shrug. "I don't know."

I take a drag of my cigarette, puffing out an O shape as I stare at the swings. "You remember when swings were the epitome of excitement?"

He glances at me then the swings and back again. "I guess."

"I remember this one time when I was maybe three, begging my mum and dad to take me to the park even though the sky was grey, and it was about to rain. They gave in." I smile at the memory. "That's when I got this." My finger runs over the scar on my forehead.

"What happened?"

"I was swinging so high I thought maybe if I let go, I might be able to fly." I shake my head with a laugh. "Damn swing flipped upside down and I faceplanted on the bark, knocked myself out." I turn my gaze on him. "But you know what? I was back on that swing a week later."

"Why are you telling me this?"

"So now you know a little more about me, maybe you'll stop acting like I'm gonna beat the shit outta you and sit down." He opens his mouth to speak but says nothing, instead, perching on the edge of the seat. "Now it's your turn."

"What?"

"Tell me something about you."

"Uh, why?"

"It's called getting to know each other."

"Um…"

I take a drag of my cigarette, the smoke curling down my throat. "You always wanted to be a doctor?"

He shrugs. "I guess."

"Shit, for someone who writes such eloquent words on paper, you're not much of a conversationalist, are ya?" I shake my head with a laugh.

He frowns. "What do you… How do you know what I write?"

Shit. I run my hand through my hair before I look at him. "Uh, I might've come across something at your place the other night." I pull the journal out from my back pocket. "This shit is really good."

"You stole my journal?" He snatches it from my hand, flipping through the pages. "How much did you read?"

"Enough to know you're chasing the wrong dream, doc."

"Writing won't pay the bills." As soon as the words leave his mouth he frowns, shaking his head as if he doesn't know where the thought came from. "It's just a hobby." He flicks the pages again. "Why me? What's your sudden interest in me?"

"I'm not gonna lie, seeing you the other night in your tighty whiteys may have influenced me some."

He scoffs. "I would never wear tighty whiteys."

"Whatever. I bet you have a whole drawer full of 'em."

"You wish."

"Maybe I do." He looks at me as though he can't comprehend what I'm saying. "What? You thought you were the only one?"

"No, I mean. Of course I'm not the only one. I just didn't know you were… you know, like me."

"Into dudes?"

He drops his gaze to his feet, his voice barely more than a whisper. "Yeah."

"It's not something I advertise, but yeah, I like guys." He nods, keeping his head down. "Your folks know?"

He shakes his head. "No. Yours?"

"Nah, not yet. Mum's kinda different, so I don't think she'd give two shits. I just figured I'd wait until there was someone worth mentioning."

"I think Mum would be okay with it too, and I've thought about telling her before, but she'd tell Dad, and he doesn't really like me much as it is. I'm in no hurry to add another reason for him to hate me."

"That why you didn't rat me out? To get back at your old man?"

"Huh. I don't know. Maybe." He turns to face me. "What about you? Why're you breaking into homes? Who're *you* getting back at?"

I drop my cigarette butt to the ground and stub it out with my foot. "It's complicated."

"Are you in trouble?"

"Why? You gonna rescue me?"
"That depends."
"On what?"
"Do you want me to?"

Chapter Ten

Alexander

Do you want me to? Who the hell am I? Hi, I'm Alex, and I'll say stupid cheesy lines like I'm in a goddamn movie to make you like me. Ugh.

The silence is almost unbearable as he stares into my eyes. I want to look away but somehow the message isn't getting through from my brain to my retinas. *He thinks you're an idiot. He's wishing he hadn't asked you here.*

"I think maybe I do."

Wait, what?

"You do?" My voice raises an octave, and I try to swallow it back.

"I mean, that's kinda why I asked you here."

The penny drops. *He needs my money, not me. Of course he doesn't want me.*

With a sigh, I pull out my wallet. "How much?"

"You think I want your money? Shit, doc, put it away." He shakes his head, reaching for his cigarettes again.

"I'm sorry, I thought… shit."

"You thought shit?" He smirks, running his hand over his head. "That what people always ask you for? Money?"

"Pretty much, yeah." In a moment of stupidity, I pinch the smoke from between his fingers and bring it to my lips, inhaling deeply. Whoever said smoking was smooth was a goddamn liar, because that shit burns all the way down. An almighty bark bubbles up from my chest and I swear I almost hack up a lung.

Leo laughs, smacking a hand to my back. The electrifying jolt of pain sends me flying to my knees on the ground.

"Shit, are you okay? I didn't mean to hit you that hard."

Bracing my hands on the ground in front of me, I suck in as much air as I can without breaking into another coughing fit. My body automatically rocks back and forth as if that action will take the searing pain away.

"Doc?"

I turn my tear-streaked face up to his. "I'm fine." My voice is strained, and it's clear I'm lying, but I try to push up to my feet anyway.

"Woah, what the hell is this, doc?" His eyes are locked on my back, and suddenly my choice of shirt doesn't seem like such a good idea. "What the fuck *is* this?" He reaches out as if he wants to touch me but doesn't know how or where.

"It's nothing. Don't worry about it." I straighten up, but his eyes remain on what I'm sure is my weeping wounds seeping through the thin material on my back.

"Your dad?" His hands ball into fists at his sides when I nod. "He beats you?" I nod again. "Your mum?"

I shake my head. "She doesn't know. She's always busy with her art, and he makes sure he doesn't do it where she can see."

"Well he's not doing a good job, because I can fucking see it, doc!" He steps closer, his hands tentatively touching the collar of my shirt.

Knowing he won't let it go, I bring my shaking fingers to my chest and begin unbuttoning my shirt. With the last button undone, I shrug my top down my arms as gently as I can manage.

With my head bowed down, I don't see his reaction, but I hear the sharp intake of breath. His hands hover above my wounds, as if perhaps he can draw the pain away, and in a way, he does just by being here. I've never shown anyone my scars before. Not a single soul. This is *my* cross to bear. Not anyone else's.

"Jesus, doc. This is fresh. He did this just now, didn't he? Just before you left." I nod, not willing to meet his eyes. "How often does this happen?"

"It varies. Sometimes he can go a few weeks without hitting me, other times he can barely last two nights."

"How long has this been going on?"

I shrug. "As long as I can remember."

"He beat you as a child?"

"It didn't start out that way. More verbal. This is a more recent development. The last few years, give or take."

"You ever fight back?"

"I've thought about it, but no. I worked out it's easier if I just take it."

He throws his hands in the air, bringing them down to rest on his head. "Fuck, man. Your dad does that to you," he points at my back, "and even though you think I'm going to do the same thing, you still come here to meet me, even asking me if *I* need to be rescued." He shakes his head. "It should be me who's rescuing you."

"You are."

He scoffs. "How?"

I swallow the lump in my throat, barely whispering the words, "By giving a shit."

Chapter Eleven

Leo

Never in my wildest dreams did I imagine his life was just as fucked up as mine. With his good looks, smarts, and wads of cash, it's easy to assume he's got his shit together, but clearly, I was wrong. His life is far from charmed, and if it wasn't for our chance encounter the other night, I would still be in the dark. Sure, shitty fathers aren't exactly a new thing; mine did a runner when Zack was just a baby. Even so, he never raised a hand to me, and for a while at least, he seemed to give a shit. But what Alex is going through? That's rough. I can't imagine how it would feel to have your father look at you in hate or use his fists to hurt you. That shit ain't right.

I came here with the intention of asking Alex to give me extra help with my essay writing, so I can pass and get into college to better myself so I can provide for Mum and Zack. She hasn't been able to hold down a job for years, and the little I bring in from our break-ins isn't sustainable. One day the law will catch up to me, and then what? Zack will be left to fend for himself while Mum sleeps the days away? Not on my watch.

But I've already been kept back a year, and I can't afford to lose another. I've got the smarts; I'm good with numbers, just the essay writing does my head in. The words jumble, and I can't get them out the way I want. Ever since I was little, words and me haven't really gelled. They said I might have some form of dyslexia or something, but it never really bothered me before. Not until I realised how important it is for my future.

In light of what I've just discovered, it seems so trivial to even ask such a thing of him. He's got enough on his plate without me adding to it.

We sit in silence. I can't think of a single thing to say to him that will make this better. What *can* you say to something like that?

"So," Alex starts, kicking his feet in the dirt. "I've made this awkward. Sorry."

"Don't. Don't ever apologise for that. For what *he* did to you" I practically growl the words through gritted teeth. "You don't ever have to hide that from me, okay?"

He looks into my eyes for the longest time before nodding his head. "Okay."

I reach out and grab his hand, giving it a squeeze. "I got your back."

His eyes drop to our joined hands and he sighs. "No one knows. You can't tell anyone. It'll just make it worse."

"I may be a petty thief, but I'm no snitch. Don't worry, you can trust me."

"Why are you doing this? Why do you care what happens to me?"

Why am *I doing this?*

"Because we've all got our demons, and sometimes having someone to share it with is the only thing that keeps you going. No one should have to suffer alone. No one."

"You don't even know me. Not really."

"I know enough." I shuffle closer, nudging his shoulder with my arm. "And like I said, that picture of you in your tighty whiteys gets my motor running."

He shakes his head with a snigger. "I don't even own a pair of tighty whiteys!"

"Sure, sure. That's what they all say."

Chapter Twelve

Alexander

Lying in bed, staring at the wall, I try to wrap my head around what happened tonight. Meeting Leo turned out to be far beyond my expectations, and in a good way. I guess we both had preconceived ideas about each other. Goes to show, you really can't judge someone until you get to know them. And Leo is someone I'd like to get to know a whole lot better. Judging by his flirtation, I think the feeling is mutual. At least, I hope it is.

Butterflies flit about in my stomach when I think about his hand holding mine. He did it so nonchalantly, like he couldn't care less who saw us together. I wish I could have that kind of confidence to just be me, the *real* me, without worrying about what my father would do or say. Living in fear is really starting to take its toll, and I'm counting down the days until I can truly be free of him.

College is just around the corner, and as excited as I am about it, I'm also a little apprehensive. For the first time in my life I'm worried about leaving. Not because of my family, but as crazy as it sounds, because of Leo. I've spent my life pretending to be someone I'm not, but with him, I don't have to. In a sad twist of fate, I've found the one person I can share everything with, just when I'm about to leave. I've never opened up to anyone like I did with him. After only talking a handful of times, he knows my deepest, darkest secrets, and it feels amazing. I didn't realise how much keeping it all bottled up inside was weighing me down. It's like he's carrying some of it for me, like I'm not alone anymore.

Leaving that behind to face the world on my own suddenly seems so daunting. I'm not so naïve to think everyone will be as accepting as Leo. The world is full of close-minded people like my father, and just like him, they can hide it well.

Of course, Leo may want to attend college too, but I can hardly expect him to follow me. It's not like we're a couple, and I don't even know what he wants to major in, if anything at all. For all I know, college might not even be on his agenda.

It occurs to me I don't know a lot about him. We never really discussed what he wanted to meet me for, and somehow the conversation always seemed to turn back to me. Am I that selfish that I have to monopolise an entire conversation?

Thinking back, perhaps I could've asked more questions, got to know him better. Instead,

I took advantage of his attention and poured my heart and soul out for him to see. Huh. Maybe I *am* selfish.

Not anymore. No. Tomorrow is another day, and I'm making it my mission to find out what makes Leo tick.

***

When I walk out the door in the morning, Leo is waiting outside, his hip pushed up against the fence with a cigarette hanging from his lips. Just seeing his grin is enough to set my heart racing, but I try to play it cool.

"Hey."

"Hey. Thought we could walk to school together." He pushes off from the fence and grabs my bag, throwing it over his shoulder. "How's the back?"

I fall into step beside him with a shrug. "Still the same."

He nods, taking a final drag on his smoke before flicking the butt to the ground. "Give me your phone." He holds his hand out, and I slap my phone down without question. After pushing a few numbers, a beep comes from his back pocket. "Now you have my number. He does it again, you call me." He holds my phone out for me but when I go to grab it he pulls it away, just out of my reach. "I mean it, doc. He so much as looks at you wrong, you let me know. I don't care what time it is. You need me, I'm there."

A rush of heat flows to my cheeks and tears prick my eyes. I've never had anyone stand up for me before. Sure, no one knows what goes on behind closed doors, but the fact he's willing to jump into the line of fire for me is enough to bring me to tears. I'm afraid to speak in case I actually do cry, so I settle for a nod as I pocket my phone.

"So, ah, you free later to help me with my English? I really need to pass, and these essays are kicking my ass."

"Yeah, sure. At the park, after school?"

"It's a date." He flashes that grin of his and again, my heart it goes a-galloping. It's impossible not to grin back at him, his smile is so infectious. "You should do that more often, you know?"

"Do what?"

"Smile." Using the tip of his finger, he raises my chin to meet his gaze. "Your whole face lights up, and you don't look like you have a stick up your ass anymore."

"Uh, thanks?" It's certainly not the nicest thing anyone has ever said to me before.

He drops his hand, tucking it in his pocket. "I'm just saying, I don't think I'd seen you smile until last night, and we've been at school together all year."

Huh. And here was me thinking he'd never noticed me before. "Well, maybe that's because I didn't have anything to smile about until last night."

Chapter Thirteen

Leo

School is pretty uneventful until last period. As we're about to get our assignments for the fortnight, a call comes over the intercom, asking me to make my way to the office. My stomach drops, and I'm filled with dread. The only times I'm called to the office are when something's happened at home. I knew I shouldn't have left Zack this morning. I was being selfish, wanting to see Alex again. We've been meeting the last few nights after school to go over my essay writing, but it's never quite enough. Seeing him in the mornings sets me up for the day, and things just seem to go smoother. At least, they had until today.

With my bag gripped firmly in my hand, I stride to the office and up to the desk. "Ah, there was a call for me to come in." I sweep my hand through my hair to rest on the back of my neck.

Mrs Rogers has that smile on her face. The one that says she pities me. "This way, dear." She stands and holds a weathered hand up to touch the small of my back as she guides me through to the guidance counsellor. I swallow back my fear.

The sound of sobbing permeates the air and I hasten my steps. "Zack!" I burst through the door without knocking, dropping to my knees and holding my arms out wide. Zack's wide eyes meet mine as he flings himself into my arms.

"S-s-s-sowwy," he hiccups, burying his face into my neck. I wrap my arms around him as tight as I can, hoping to bring him some sort of comfort.

"It's okay, buddy." I kiss his tear-streaked cheek before turning my attention to Mr Falkner. "What happened?" My voice cracks, announcing my fear to the room.

"Why don't we take a seat over here." He gestures to the couch by the window. It's then I notice the cop standing with his arms folded in front of him, his hat dangling.

This can't be good.

"Come on." I hoist Zack onto my hip as I stand and make my way over to the seat. His tiny arms pull tight against my neck as if he's afraid to let go. "It's okay, buddy. We're gonna be okay." I eye the cop, knowing my words are lies.

"Mrs Rogers, why don't you see if we have something for Zack to play with?" Mr Falkner says. "Maybe something to colour?"

Zack's head lifts a fraction, and I force a smile on my face. "That'd be fun, eh, Zack? You love colouring."

He sniffs and wipes his arm under his nose. "Y-y-you gots w-w-wacing caws to dwaw?"

Mrs Rogers holds her hand out to him. "I'm sure we can find some racing cars. Why don't you come and help me?"

He bites his lips, peering into my eyes. "It's okay, buddy, you can go with her. She's a friend."

He slides his hands up to my cheeks and rests his forehead against mine. "You b-be otay?" he whispers.

"Yeah, buddy. I'll be okay. I'm going to be right here, talking with Mr Falkner."

"Otay." He pulls back, wiping the tears from his eyes. "I be good. I be vewy quiet." His voice wavers on those last words.

I kiss his cheek. "I know, Zack. It's okay. You're not in trouble."

"O-otay." His bottom lip drops and quivers. I want to scoop him up and take him away from this nightmare. He must be so scared.

Lowering him to the floor, I ruffle his hair and give Mrs Rogers a nod. She holds her hand out again and he tentatively takes it. He takes a quick glance over his shoulder, but I wave him on with a smile. "Way you go, buddy. Show Mrs Rogers how good you are at colouring."

I watch him leave, wishing I could be following behind. When the door closes, I huff out a breath, dropping my head. "Is she okay?"

Thick as Thieves

Chapter Fourteen

Alexander

I'm worried about Leo. When his name was called over the intercom before the end of class, his face paled and I knew it wouldn't be good news. Mrs Rogers won't tell me a damn thing though, she just keeps playing with some kid on the floor.

I'm not leaving though. Not until I know he's okay.

The door to Mr Falkner's office swings open and Leo steps out with his bag slung over his shoulder and a police officer trailing behind him. My heart pounds at the thought of him being arrested. *Have they finally caught up to him and his friends?*

"My door is always open, Leo." Mr Falkner nods at Leo and holds his hand out for the officer to shake.

"Thank you, Sir." He steps forward, his eyes searching the room until they land on the little boy with Mrs Rogers. "Hey, buddy." He crouches down, his arms extended. "What did you draw?"

"A dinosaw! And wook!" He holds his tiny fist out for Leo to see.

"Wow! You must have been extra specially good to get a stamp. High five, buddy." He lifts his hand in the air and the little boy leaps up to slap it.

"We go home now?"

"Uh…" Leo looks to the officer who nods. "Sure. We can go home." He stands, lifting the little boy into his arms. I step away from the wall and into his line of sight. The look on his face is one I've never seen before. Red-rimmed eyes filled with sorrow meet mine, making me want to run to him and wrap him in my arms.

I mouth the words, *Are you okay?* He nods, sucking a breath in through his nose before huffing it out. I know it's a lie, but I won't push for answers. Not with little ears listening.

With his thumb in his mouth, the little boy nuzzles into Leo's neck and for the first time I see the similarity between them. Same blue eyes framed with dark lashes, same curve to their lips. *Brothers.*

"Alex." Hearing my name on his lips gives me a shiver. "You didn't have to come."

"I know. I wanted to make sure you were okay." I eye the officer still talking with Mr Falkner. "Are you in trouble?" I whisper.

He follows my gaze then shakes his head. "Nah, nothing like that."

"You wanna talk about it?"

His eyes drift to the bundle in his arms and he shakes his head again. "Not right now."

"Okay." I rock back on my heels. *Should I stay, or should I go?*

The decision is made for me. "You could walk with us. If you want." He shrugs as if he doesn't care, but one look at his eyes tells me it's quite the opposite. *He needs me.*

"Yeah, sure." I hoist my bag up from the floor and just like he did this morning, he grabs it and swings it onto his back with his own. "You don't have to do that. I can carry it."

"I know. I want to." His tone brooks no argument, so I shove my hands in my pockets and fall into step beside him. Even with a kid on his hip and two backpacks on his back, Leo strides forward as if the extra weight barely registers.

I watch him whisper something to his brother to make him giggle, and I can't help the smile that forms on my lips. He's so good with him. It's something I never would have expected had we not met up that night. This softer side isn't something he displays at school. I'd even hazard to guess he keeps it hidden from his usual crowd too. Somehow it doesn't quite fit with the thieving and tomfoolery I'd always pegged him with.

He's sweet and caring, with a fierce loyalty. In a way, his interest in me makes more sense now. With what I divulged the other night, I've appealed to his base instinct; to protect.

A pudgy finger reaches across my face to press my nose. "Boop." Growing up the way I did, I missed out on silly games like this, so I do the only thing I can think of. I 'boop' his nose right back.

He grins and waves at me. "Hi."

"Hi. I'm Alex. What's your name?"

"Zack. And dis Weo." He thumps his palm on Leo's chest.

"He knows who I am, buddy. Alex is my—"

"Boyfwiend," Zack interrupts.

"Uh…" My cheeks heat as I lift my gaze to Leo's. He looks amused, and right now, I'll take that over the look of despair he was wearing earlier. "Yeah, sure. I'm his boyfriend."

"I knowed dis." He taps his finger against the top of his head.

"You're pretty smart, huh?"

"Uh-huh. I knowed lots." He pauses, slowly counting his fingers before holding three in the air. "I dis many yeaws."

"You're three?" I ask, throwing a hand to my chest.

He nods. "Uh-huh."

With a whistle and a shake of my head, I say, "I thought you were at least ten."

"No!" Zack giggles, shaking his head from side to side.

"I bet your parents are really smart too, huh?" I grin. "Probably runs in the family." I don't notice at first, but Leo's step falters and Zack goes quiet. They're looking at each other, their eyes speaking volumes, and I know I've put my foot in it.

"I beed vewy quiet," Zack whispers, and Leo nods.

"I know, buddy. It's not your fault."

Shit.

"Sorry, I wasn't thinking. I didn't mean to upset anyone." I rest my hand on the small of Zack's back, meeting Leo's eyes.

"It's okay." His lips pull up in a half smile before he turns to Zack. "Hey, how 'bout we get some ice cream?"

Thick as Thieves

Chapter Fifteen

Leo

Once Zack is settled on the couch with a scoop of goody-goody-gumdrops and his favourite cartoon, I nudge Alex into the kitchen and out of earshot. I feel like such an ass for not telling him what's going on. It wasn't fair for me to expect him to know not to mention Mum.

"About before—" I hold my hand up to stop him.

"Don't." Raking my hand through my hair, I rest my hip against the counter and take a deep breath. "Everything is just really fucked up right now, and I stupidly wanted to pretend it wasn't. Just be us and Zack, ya know?"

"Okay."

How do I explain to someone who doesn't know what it's like? Where do I even begin?

He reaches across and takes my hand in his, his thumb rubbing circles across my skin.

"Are you okay?"

I stare at our hands, fighting the urge to fall apart in front of him. I'm meant to be the strong one. My life is so different to what he's used to, and with what I know of his life, I don't want to burden him with my problems.

My mother loves me, I know this, but it's hard for me to hold onto that feeling sometimes. When she has one of her episodes, it makes me want to shake her. To scream, "We're right here! See us!" But it would be no use. She sees what her mind allows her to see. She gets stuck inside her own head and can't find her way back out. No matter what I do or say, she becomes lost.

"Leo?" Alex tentatively brings his hand to my cheek and I turn into the soft caress with my eyes closed. Just that simple touch gives me the courage to speak.

"My mum is bipolar." I swallow back the lump in my throat and force myself to continue. "She sometimes has these episodes where she can't get herself out of bed for days on end. It's like she goes to a dark place inside her mind and can't find her way back out."

Alex slides his hand up my arm, his eyes searching mine. "That must be really hard for you." I nod and shrug my shoulders. "Is she having one now? Is that why Zack was at school today?"

Again, I nod. "Yeah." The word catches in my throat. "She, uh…" *Shit, this is harder than I thought it'd be.* "She, uh… she tried to…" I turn my head away so he doesn't see the tears forming, but he's on his feet and moving around the counter to wrap me in his arms before I can stop him.

"I'm so sorry, Leo." I bury my head in his shoulder, my fists gripping his waist so I don't hurt his back. He holds me tight, helping me to stay upright when all I want to do is crumple to the floor. It's so hard to be strong all the time.

He holds me until my tears have dried and I can breathe again. I haven't cried like that since I was a child. Having a mother with bipolar meant I had to grow up pretty quickly and learn how to fend for myself. I've tried to spare Zack the same fate, but after today, I don't know what lies in our future.

When I pull away from Alex's embrace, my body instantly misses his touch. I can see he has questions, so I take his hand and bring it to my lips. "What do you want to know?"

His eyes widen, and he shakes his head. "No, it's okay. You've been through enough without me prying further."

"Honestly, I can handle it."

His teeth pull his bottom lip in as he weighs up what's on his mind. "Is she, um…"

"Alive?" He nods. "Yeah. Just. She's in the hospital."

He glances at the door towards where Zack sits, and I know what he's thinking.

"Yes, he was here when she did it. The neighbour found him playing in the yard by himself. She's been around since he was a baby so she knows what goes on around here. She looks out for him when I'm at school and Mum is… incapacitated." I clear my throat as a fresh lot of tears threaten. "If she hadn't taken him home for a snack before checking on Mum, he would've walked in to something I don't think he'd recover from." I turn my gaze on him. "I don't even know if *I* can face it, but I have to. I can't let him see where…"

"I'll do it."

I shake my head. "No. Alex, I can't ask you to do that."

He takes my hand and leads me through the door, pointing at Zack. "That little boy in there needs you. And you need him too. Go and give him a hug, let him know you're here. Let me take care of this for you."

Chapter Sixteen

Alexander

This is so much bigger than I imagined. My mind went into overdrive when I thought he was being arrested, but this? This is heart-breaking. It's devastating. It's the kind of thing you expect to see on the TV, not in your own home. And Leo has been dealing with this his whole life. Never knowing what he's going to get when he comes home from school. That has to be scary.

To have a cop show up at school with your baby brother to tell you your mother tried to take her own life? That's next level. That's beyond even what I can comprehend. I can't even begin to imagine what's going through his mind right now, but cleaning up her… cleaning up what she did, shouldn't have to fall on his shoulders. I may not know what I'm diving into here, but I'll be damned if I'm going to leave Leo to deal with it on his own.

As I make my way down the hallway, a metallic aroma permeates the air, and I know I'm close. The only closed door beckons to me, drawing me closer. This is it. This is where she did it.

With a trembling hand, I grip the handle and push it open. The tiny bathroom is much like any other; stark white walls, ceramic clawfoot bath and single vanity. A red smear trails over the edge of the tub, and I brace myself for what hides behind the curtain.

Deep breath. You can do it.

***

The mind is a complex thing. It can make you see things that aren't there, and it can help you pretend things aren't as they seem. Pulling back that curtain had been something out of a horror movie, but knowing I couldn't let Leo see it, I somehow compartmentalised it and got the job done. You'd never know anything had happened in there. And he'll never have to deal with the imagery such a scene can create.

With the smell of bleach in the air, I pull the door closed and pad back down the hallway. Zack is snuggled into Leo's side, his eyes closed. They look so at peace, I almost don't want to interrupt. I slip in behind the couch and slide my hand down his shoulder. "All done," I whisper. "I'm going to head off before my father goes ballistic." Before I can talk myself out of it, I lean down and press my cheek to his. "Text me later, if you want."

His hand cups my cheek. "Thank you. I don't think I could've faced that."

"You've got my back, and I've got yours."

"Forever and always." My heart soars. Who'd have thought that catching a thief in my boxer briefs could end up being the best thing to ever happen to me? I certainly didn't see it coming, but I wouldn't give it up for all the tea in China. For all our differences, deep down, we're just two guys wading through our screwed up lives, trying not to drown.

***

"What time do you call this?" My father greets me at the door with his arms folded across his chest. I knew I was pushing it for time, but for the first time in my life, I don't care. There's nothing he can do to me that will rival what Leo is dealing with. Nothing.

When I go to step past him, he shifts, blocking my entry. "I asked you a question."

Squaring my shoulders, I face him. "Sorry. I lost track of time." My jaw grinds as I force the words out.

"And?"

"And it won't happen again."

"You're damn right it won't. There will be no skiving off. You'll never make it as a surgeon if you can't manage your time efficiently." *Says the man who couldn't hack the pressure of medical school and dropped out.*

"Like I said. It won't happen again."

He leans in, his nose almost touching mine, and I can smell the alcohol on his breath. "It won't happen again, what?" He overenunciates the T, making me flinch.

"It won't happen again… *Sir.*" The word tastes bitter in my mouth.

His lips curl up in a sneer. "That's right." He steps back, looking me up and down. "Go and get cleaned up. Dinner is almost ready."

Gladly. Anything to be away from him.

Thick as Thieves

Chapter Seventeen

Leo

I don't think I've ever seen the bathroom look so clean before. The ceramic is so shiny I can almost make out my reflection as I stare blankly. Zack needs to have a bath, but I can't bring myself to turn the taps knowing she was here. Knowing this was the spot she decided she couldn't go on.

I don't even know how to feel right now. Part of me is angry and hurt that she'd leave us on a whim. Yes, deep down I know it's more than that for her, but the selfish part inside me wants to know why we weren't enough of a reason for her to want to fight it.

The rest of me is just fucking tired. Tired of being the glue that holds us together. Tired of having to be the strong one. This afternoon with Alex was the first time I've let go in a long time, and it felt amazing. To have someone take the reigns and let me fall apart was worth more than any takings from a heist. It was freeing. For a while at least.

With Alex gone and only my three-year-old brother for company, the reality of our situation smacks me full force in the face. I don't know how long she'll be in the hospital for, but I doubt she'll be home any time soon. She needs the kind of help I can't provide for her here. What worries me is what will happen to Zack. I'm no longer a child in the eyes of the law, but where does that leave him? Can I keep him with me or will he be taken to a foster home? The thought of being separated from him is like a knife straight to the heart.

"Fuck." I pull the door closed and slide down to the floor, my head in my hands. *Why'd she have to do this?*

Two feet in mismatched socks appear in front of me, and two hands slide around to cup my cheeks. "You otay?" His eyes brim with tears and all my anger drains away.

I pull him into my arms. "I'm okay, buddy. Just a little bit sad."

He nods then squirms out of my embrace to run down the hall to his room. When he reappears, he has his worn teddy in his hands. The stinky bear is thrust into my face. "Hewe. You can hold Lawwy if you want. He make me not sad."

This kid.

"Thanks, buddy." My voice cracks as I take his offering and squeeze the bear who's seen better days to my chest. "That's really thoughtful of you. But won't you need him to go to sleep?"

He purses his lips as if thinking. "I be otay. You needs him maw."

"You're the best, you know that? And I think Alex was right. You're pretty smart." I pull him in and ruffle his hair. "What do you say we get a cloth and give you a quick wash in the sink before bed?"

"No bath?"

"No bath. We can pretend you're a giant and the sink is a lake. You can even grab a boat to play with if you like."

His eyes widen at the idea of playing a game. "Weally?"

"Sure. I'll go fill up the kitchen sink and grab a towel. You go find a toy boat."

"Otay!" He runs back to his room while I pull myself up from the floor. No time for wallowing. Zack needs me to be strong, and I refuse to let him down.

Chapter Eighteen

Alexander

"Hey." I rush down the path. "I wasn't expecting to see you this morning. Is everything okay?"

"Yeah, everything's fine. I asked Mrs Hyde to watch Zack so I could go to school." Leo grabs my bag and slings it over his shoulder.

"Is that a good idea? Maybe you should take some time off." My fingers itch to touch him but I don't dare do it so close to home.

"I just need something to take my mind off everything, ya know? I can't be in that house any longer. It's too much right now." He nudges my arm with his elbow. "And if I'm completely honest, being with you calms me."

"Yeah?" My chest fills with pride. "I'm not gonna lie, being with you scares the shit out of me." He stops walking and stares at me. "I-I mean in a good way." *Shit, I'm screwing this up.* "This thing we have," I wave my hand between us. "It's like nothing I've ever experienced before. It's like you're the first person to ever really see me, and, I dunno, I feel like maybe it's the same for you?" His eyes bore into mine, and suddenly I feel like I've read this all wrong. "Or not. I mean, whatever." I avert my eyes and start walking.

"Wait." He grabs my arm, sliding his hand down to take mine. "I *do* see you. And you see so much more in me than anyone ever has. I'm not just a stupid thug when I'm with you. And I like that. I like that so damn much. Hell,

I feel like I can move mountains as long as you're by my side."

Before I realise what I'm doing, my hand is caressing his cheek. "But you could anyway. You're the strongest person I know."

"Pfft." He shoves his hands in his pockets. "Are you kidding? I fell apart in your arms last night. That's not strong."

"It takes strength to let go and embrace your feelings." My thumb runs across his cheek, and his eyes meet mine before darting to my lips as he steps in closer. My heart nearly beats out of my chest as I realise what he's about to do. And, God do I want his lips on mine, just… not out here… in public. I take a step back, my head flicking side to side to see if anyone is watching.

His face drops. "Oh, I get it."

"Leo, I'm sorry. It's not that I don't want to."

"No, I understand. It takes strength to embrace your feelings, just not when you're in public and word could get to Daddy."

"Leo—"

"It's cool." He hands me my backpack. "I've gotta get going. Think I *will* give school a miss today." He sniffs and turns on his heels, leaving me feeling like a jackass.

Fuck! Why'd I have to pull away?

Everything was going great, and then I went and ruined it by being too scared to show him how I truly feel. *Good one, Alexander.*

The walk to school is slow as I rack my brains, trying to come up with a way to make this up to him. The more I think about it, the more I think I should just front up and tell my father I'm gay. Fuck the consequences. Taking a beating is nothing compared to what Leo is going through right now. He needs me, and I let him down. If he can be honest about his feelings, then so can I. I just hope I live to tell the tale.

Chapter Nineteen

Leo

I'm an asshole. Plain and simple. I know exactly why he doesn't want to come out, and yet I tried to force him to anyway to fuel my ego and make me feel better for five minutes. It's not his fault my life is so fucked up. I should be glad he even wants to give me the time of day, I mean, I broke into his home and stole his journal for fuck's sake. I haven't exactly given him reason to want to hang around, but somehow, he's still here. Or, he was, at least. Now I've probably fucked it all up and sent him running for the hills.

Stupid, stupid, stupid.

What the hell was I thinking? Packing a sad because he wasn't ready for a PDA. Truth be told, I don't even know if I'm ready myself. I got caught up in the moment and before I knew it, I'd put myself out there, going in for the first kiss. I knew it, even as I leaned in, that he wasn't ready, but I kept going anyway, desperately seeking the peace that comes with his touch. He calms the storms in my mind with just a look, a simple touch. And like an addict, I crave it.

Look where that got me. Sitting on a park bench, alone, surrounded by cigarette butts, kicking my feet against the dirt. I should pick Zack up, but I can't face Mrs Hyde right now. She'll try and convince me to go see Mum. I know I should, but seeing her strapped to a hospital bed with bandaged wrists will only make it more real. And that's a reality I really don't want to face. I know what comes next.

They'll put her in some rehab facility until her meds kick in and she can be trusted to be at home with us again. But how can I ever trust that she won't try it again? That next time she won't put Zack in danger? And what if she refuses to take her meds? Then what? How do I force a grown woman to do that?

Dropping my head into my hands, I hiss out a breath. "Fuck." This is more than I need to deal with when exams are looming. How am I meant to pass now? How am I meant to get through this so I can provide a better life for Zack? *How the fuck do I do this?*

Tears spring to my eyes, and I fucking hate how weak I feel. I don't cry. I don't have meltdowns. I get shit done. I look after my own, and I get shit done. *So why the fuck can't I breathe right now?*

I press the heel of my hands into my eyes as if it will stop the tears. "Fuck!" I draw in a ragged breath and curl my body even further down between my knees. No matter how hard I try, I just can't seem to get enough air into my lungs.

Something drops by my feet and two arms entwine themselves around me. "Shh, it's okay. Everything's gonna be okay."

Alex.

"I can't... I can't..." The words won't come out but he understands. He drops to his knees in front of me. His hands move to my face, cupping my cheeks and forcing me to look him in the eyes. I'm drowning in a sea of whiskey and he's my life raft.

"You can. You can do this. Breathe with me." He takes a deep breath in through his nose and out through his mouth, and as I watch him, my chest loosens and I'm able to suck in a shallow breath. "That's it. Just breathe. Do it with me. In... Out."

His voice, his touch, his very presence is enough to pull me back from the precipice. With his hands still firmly wrapped around my face, he draws me in, resting his forehead against mine. "I've got you. Forever and always."

My heart thumps in my chest, but for an entirely different reason. His lips are a hair's breadth away from mine. All I'd need to do is tilt up a little and they would meet. I close my eyes and imagine how they would feel.

"I'm sorry," he whispers. "I never should have let you walk away."

I shake my head. "No. I never should have put pressure on you. That wasn't fair of me. I'm sorry."

"You don't have to apologise for how you feel for me, because I can guarantee you, I feel the same way."

He pulls back ever so slightly, then slowly leans forward, pressing his lips to mine. When I bring my hands up to slide behind his neck and into his hair, he lets out a soft moan. I drop to my knees, sliding one hand down his back and pulling his body against mine. I run my tongue along the seam of his lips, and he moans again, giving me entry. His hands travel down to my chest, his fingers hovering above my heart. I'm sure he can feel how fast it's racing, how his touch alone affects me.

When we come up for air, his smile is more radiant than the sun, and it's easy to forget what brought us here in the first place. His eyes are hooded as they dart to my lips and back again. "That was—"

"Amazing? Mind-blowing? The best you've ever had?" I grin, pressing my lips to his once more.

He chuckles. "All of the above and more." Colour fills his cheeks as he looks away with a bite of his lip. *Surely that wasn't...*

"Was that your first kiss?" The colour deepens, and I pull his face back to look at me. "I was your first?" When he nods, I can't help the feeling of elation that courses through my body, making me grin like a fool.

"Like that idea, huh?" He grins back, shaking his head.

"I mean, what's not to like? I'm the first, guy to ever touch these lips... and I'll be the last." I run my thumb across his plump bottom lip. "That's pretty fucking special if you ask me."

"First and last, eh? You seem pretty sure of yourself," he teases.

"Oh I am. Forever and always, baby, remember?"

Thick as Thieves

Chapter Twenty

Alexander

"You sure about this? We can still go to mine if you've changed your mind." Leo says as I open the gate to let us through. "It's not too late."

"Stop worrying. My parents are at work. We'll be fine to hang here for a few hours." I unlock the front door and disable the alarm. "Come on. I'd show you around, but I think you already know the place."

"Oh, ha-ha. Ladies and gentlemen, Alex the kidder." He sweeps his hand out in front of him like a circus ringmaster.

I lead him down the hallway to my room. He makes a beeline for my bed, bouncing on the edge. "Cushy."

"Yeah." Now that he's here, in my room, I don't know how to act. Why do I feel so awkward all of a sudden?

Perhaps because the hot guy you just kissed is sitting on your bed waiting for you to join him? Yup. That'll do it.

"We don't have to do anything, you know?" *Am I that obvious?* "We can just talk."

"I know. I'm just… this is the first time I've ever had anyone in my room before. I don't really know what to do."

He pats the mattress beside him. "You can start by sitting down. You're making *me* nervous."

"Okay." I join him on the bed.

"Better?"

"Mmhmm." *Can he hear my heart beating through my chest?*

He takes my hand, sliding his fingers between mine, and I swear the pounding kicks up a notch. "You know, of all the months I've known you, I don't think I've ever seen you skip class before. It's not very becoming of a doctor." He nudges my shoulder. "Why'd you come back?"

I peek up at him. "Maybe I'm having second thoughts on medical school?"

"Yeah?"

"Yeah… And… maybe I didn't want to be another person letting you down." With our fingers still entwined, I pull his hand to my lap. "I made my mind up. I'm going to tell him."

"You don't have to do that."

"I know." I shift my body to face him. "I'm tired of pretending to be someone I'm not."

"But," his eyes dart to my back, "aren't you scared he'll hurt you?"

I shrug. "A little. But when you walked away this morning, I realised nothing could hurt more than disappointing you." My finger trails down his jaw. "Not even a beating from him."

He shakes his head. "I don't know, Alex. I don't want you to get hurt because of me. I can be your dirty little secret for a few more months." He grins. "We can wait."

"No. We can't." I bring his hand to my lips, kissing his fingers. "I don't want to wait. You said this morning that you feel like you can move mountains with me by your side, well it's the same for me. I feel like I can do anything as long as you're with me." A smile forms on my lips. "You know, when I came home the other night, I stood up to him for the first time in my life. And it felt *good*."

"Shit, why didn't you tell me? Did he hurt you?"

I shake my head. "Nope. Not this time."

"You've got some balls." He chuckles, nudging my shoulder again. "I think I'm a bad influence on you. Next thing you know, you'll be thieving alongside me."

"Who knows, maybe I'll steal your heart like you stole mine." I peek up at him with a grin.

"Jesus, how long you been waiting to use that line?" The laughter in his voice warms my heart.

"Too much? How about this then? As long as you're with me, I'll do just about anything."

He whistles. "Anything, huh?"

"Why do I get the feeling I'm going to regret saying that?"

"How about we get you a pair of those tighty whiteys? Ya know, start small?"

"Nothing small about what I'm packing."

Leo throws his head back and laughs. "Fuck I'm glad I broke into your home."

"I'm fucking glad too." He stares at me with wide eyes and I can't help but poke my tongue out. "What can I say? You bring out a different side of me."

"I'm beginning to like this other side. A lot." He wraps his hand around the back of my neck and crushes his lips to mine. This time it's far from soft and gentle. It's an outpouring of our souls, binding us together. We're so caught up in each other, neither one of us notices my door creak open.

"What. The. Fuck!"

We break apart, leaping to our feet.

"Dad, I-I can explain." Caught unawares, my mind instantly falls back into a defensive stance. A quick glance at Leo has me pushing that down and bringing out the new and improved Alex. I square my shoulders and take hold of his hand.

My father's eyes flick to our sign of solidarity then return to mine with a blaze of fury alight in them. "You're a fucking pansy?"

The way he spits the word makes me flinch, but I refuse to let him scare me. "I'm no pansy. I'm gay." I turn to smile at Leo. "And this is my boyfriend."

"Your…?" As his head flits between the two of us, he resembles one of those clowns at a carnival, the ones you slot balls into. It would be comical if inside I wasn't shaking. "Get out!" he roars, one fat finger pointing at the door.

We both take a step forward, but my father shoves his hand against my chest. "Not you. You stay." He turns to Leo. "You, get the hell out of my house."

"With all due respect, Sir—"

"Am I not speaking English? I said get. Out." He stands over Leo, his face red and spittle hanging from his lip.

Leo stands taller, his eyes never leaving my father's. "I'm not leaving him here with *you*."

I tug on his hand. "Leo, it's okay. You don't need to stay."

"I'm not leaving you." He turns to meet my pleading gaze. "Forever and always, remember?"

All it takes is that split second for him to look away, and my father lunges. His hands wrap around Leo's neck as he forces him backwards. Leo's hands fly up to pry his fingers away, but they won't budge, and his face is turning red.

"No! Get off him!" I jump, throwing myself on my father's back. My hands find their way around his throat and I pull with all my might. His grip on Leo falters, and he swings his body to the side, throwing me against the wall. I cry out as my back erupts in pain.

Rubbing his neck, he storms over to me, hauling me from the ground and pinning my chest to the wall. "Fucking queer. I knew there was something wrong with you." He grabs a handful of my hair and wrenches backwards before smashing my head into the wall. My ears ring and lights flash in front of my eyes, but I force a smile on my lips just to spite him. "Get that fucking smile off your face, you filthy piece of shit."

A roar comes from behind, and my arms are freed. When I turn around, all I see is a blur of fists and legs as Leo wrestles my father to the ground. "The only filthy piece of shit here, is you!" His fist pounds into my father's nose, again and again. "What kind of a man beats up on his kid? Alex is more man than you'll *ever* be." With one final punch, he pushes off the floor, his chest heaving. Stepping over my father's body, he rushes to me, his eyes searching my face. "Are you okay?"

I stare at the body on the floor. For so long he's been my tormentor, my nightmare. And now look at him.

"Alex?" Leo's hands cup my face and draw my attention back to him. "I'm so sorry. I know he's your old man, but I just couldn't let him hurt you anymore."

Tears spring to my eyes as I look at this guy who's flipped my world upside down but somehow set it right. Bringing my hands up to clasp his, I shake my head. "I'm not sorry."

A groan sounds from the floor, and Leo pushes me behind him as my father rolls to his side. "No son of mine is going to run around town like a fucking fairy." He spits a wad of blood at our feet.

Stepping out from behind, I stare down at him with pity. "Fine by me. You haven't been a father in my eyes in a long time." I grab my bag and swipe my journal from my bedside table. "Come on, Leo."

"Where the fuck do you think you're going?"

"Anywhere you're not."

"Wiseass. You walk out that door, don't bother showing your face around here again. You disgust me."

"Believe me, the feeling is mutual." I march towards the door and my impending freedom with a smile on my face.

Always needing to have the last word, my father follows, sneering, "Good luck getting into medical school without my money paying your way."

I stop with my hand on the doorframe and turn to face him. "I never wanted to be a doctor anyway. That was *your* dream, and my excuse to get away from you." I look him up and down with contempt. "I tried so hard to get you to love me, but I see now, you're incapable of loving anything but yourself."

"Love doesn't pay the bills."

"Maybe not, but it's worth more than anything money can buy." I turn to Leo and hold my hand out to him. "And I'll choose love over money every time."

Thick as Thieves

Chapter Twenty-one

Leo

With no more than the clothes on his back and his schoolbag in his hand, Alex strides out the door and down the path without a second thought. I follow behind, keeping an eye on the entrance to make sure Mr Van der Kley doesn't come after us.

"You sure you want to do this?" I ask, not because I think he should stay, but because I don't want him to regret anything. The life he's leaving and the life he's choosing are polar opposites. *I'll choose love over money every time.* Noble, yes, but spoken like someone who's never had to want for anything a day in his life. I hope he realises how hard it's going to be.

He stops when we reach the gate, his eyes raking over the two-storey building he once called home. "I've never been more sure of anything in my life." With one last sweep over the place, he gives me a shy smile and tugs on my hand. "I don't know how I'll pay my way, but… You feel like a houseguest?"

How can I possibly say no to that face? "Are you kidding? Like I'd let you go anywhere else." I grin, letting my eyes roam over his body. "I may call on you for *other* means of payment though."

Colour fills his cheeks, and he chuckles. "I'm sure we can come up with some kind of arrangement."

I grab his bag and swing my arm around his shoulders. "I mean, I wouldn't say no to you walking around in just those tighty whiteys we talked about. Maybe a tighty whitey dance?"

He shoves my chest. "You and those bloody tighty whiteys!"

"What can I say?" I shrug, pulling a cigarette out of my pocket and lighting it. "I think you'd look hot in them. All white and… tight." A puff of smoke curls from my lips as my eyes land on the bulge between his legs.

"Maybe we could get matching pairs." He waggles his eyebrows at me.

"Ha! Not a chance in hell."

"It was worth a shot." His smile fades. "Seriously though, I know it's not going to be easy, and I want you to know, I don't expect you to support me. I'll drop out, get a job or something."

I wave my hand through the air. "Don't even worry about that right now. We'll figure something out." I veer off the path towards the park bench. "What about college and shit?"

"Ugh, I have no idea. Unless there's some sort of scholarship, I doubt I'm going to be able to go. I don't think they'll loan money to a homeless kid."

"You're not homeless."

"You know what I mean." He plonks himself down on the bench, his arm stretched out across the back. "Now that I don't have to break my back studying, I guess I'll have time to write. Maybe I'll pen the next bestselling novel." He chuckles, as if he doesn't believe he could actually do it.

"I reckon that's a pretty solid idea. It's a lot better than how I make money." I bump my elbow into his arm. "Maybe I could be your muse. You could write about a petty thief with buns of steel."

He holds his hands in the air, as if reading a sign. "I can see it now, The Tighty Whitey's Heist."

This guy. I throw my head back and laugh. "You're never gonna be the next Shakespeare with a title like that."

"Maybe a little less Shakespeare, a little more EL James." He flicks his wrist and makes a whipping sound. "Tighty Whiteys and all things Spicy."

I whistle. "Hell, I'd read that."

"Of course you would. Narcissist." He pokes his tongue between his teeth, drawing my attention back to his mouth. His damn near perfect mouth that has me mesmerised. And when his tongue darts out to run along his bottom lip, a groan slips out. "See something you like?" His smirk is my undoing.

"Damn right I do." Gripping the back of his neck, I crush my lips to his. His fingers slide into my hair as his lips part on a sigh, giving me access. My tongue follows the same path his had not so long ago, savouring the taste before plunging in and exploring. His shirt bunches in my hands as I clutch him to me, trying to close the distance between us. If I had my way, we'd be in a much less public place, wearing a lot less clothes. But we're not, we're at the park, and Zack will be wondering where I am soon. With that in mind, I pull back, planting one last kiss on his lips and pressing my forehead to his.

"God, I'm gonna love waking up to *that* every day."

I chuckle. "I can think of some other things you'll *love* waking up to."

"I don't doubt it." He threads his fingers with mine. "Hey, um, I ah, was thinking, ya know, about the whole money thing."

"Mmm."

"What if I came on a job with you?"

I jerk back, frowning. "Why would you want to do that?"

He shrugs. "I don't know. I thought it might be kinda fun. And I could help. You know, earn my keep." There's a sparkle in his eyes as he speaks, and I'm reminded of that night and the way he looked at me. All this time I'd thought it was me who'd had that effect on him, but perhaps it really was the thrill of the unexpected.

I rake a hand through my hair. "Are you serious?"

"I won't get in the way, I promise. I'll do whatever you tell me to." He flattens his hand and holds it to his forehead in a salute. "I'll even call you," he pauses, wiggling his eyebrow, "Drill Sergeant."

I can barely hold it together. "Drill Sergeant, eh?" I snigger. "I could get used to that."

"So that's a yes?" I quirk my brow at him, and he lowers his voice, his eyes hooded. "Is that a yes, Drill Sergeant?"

"That depends. Will you drop and give me twenty?"

"Whatever you say, Drill Sergeant."

Epilogue

Alexander

"You ready?" Leo's palm slaps down on my shoulder, his eyes gleaming in the pale glow of the street lamp. "It's not too late to back out."

"He's not backing out. He wouldn't do that to you." Skeet rounds the corner, joining us in the shadows.

"Of course he wouldn't. He's one of us now. No going back." Mario steps up to the corner, his too-big jacket hanging off his shoulders. "Anyway, this should be a walk in the park after last night."

"I thought last night went well," Leo says, brushing his hand down my chest with a smile.

"Yeah, if awkward silences are your thing." Meeting his mum hadn't gone quite how I'd hoped. In hindsight, mentioning me moving in before she came home might have been a good idea.

"She'll get over it." He grins, offering me his hand. "Shall we?"

"We shall." Taking his hand, I raise my eyes to the bright lights flashing at the entrance to the end-of-year formal. The theme is Hollywood, and the committee went all out with red carpets and media lights. Of course, red carpets call for suits, and Leo looks awfully dapper in his navy-blue thrift shop purchase. I even managed to convince him to wear a tie by promising he could use it in the bedroom with me after.

"Come on, let's get this show on the road." Skeet claps his hands and stalks forward, his baby-blue suit jacket flapping behind him.

"Ladies!" With arms outstretched, he gathers two giggling girls into his side, flashing a grin over his shoulder at us. "This song ain't gonna dance to itself."

"Aww, shit, you can't have both, Skeet. Sharing's caring." Mario runs to catch up to him, leaving us standing at the edge.

"Looks like a full house."

"It sure does."

"All the senior year will be in there."

"Yup."

"If you're not ready, we can just go back home."

"No." I shake my head. "I want to do this. No more hiding."

He gives my hand a squeeze. "I've got your back."

"And I've got yours."

"Forever and always, baby."

Thick as Thieves

Cyan Tayse

𝓐cknowledgements

Firstly, thank you to you, the reader, for taking a chance on my story. Alex and Leo have fast become my new favourite couple, and I hope you enjoyed reading their tale as much as I enjoyed telling it.

As always, Trina, thank you for making my words shine. I couldn't do this without you!

Nicole, thank you for being my sounding board and cheerleader. Our chats are what help me get through!

Launa and Theresa, thank you for pushing me and pimping my work out everywhere. I love you guys!

Thick as Thieves

Other Books by Cyan Tayse

Pocket Rocket novellas

Have you Ever…?
Blank Canvas

Thick as Thieves

About Cyan Tayse

Cyan Tayse is the pen name of a multi-genre author based in New Zealand. After a lot of coaxing from friends, she decided to embark on a journey of discovery. Yes, that's right, she embraced her desire to right things a little different to her usual, thus the Pocket Rocket and Brief Encounters novellas were born.

Cyan can often be found lurking on social media, and she loves to hear from fellow authors and readers.

Thick as Thieves